A

STORY

FOR

BEDTiME

By

Cornelius Clarke

Illustrations by
C.C, Niamh Clarke & Tara Clarke

For

Caitlin, Tara and Niamh

A special thank you to Niamh and Tara for their contributions to the stories and illustrations.

Also, a thank you to Caitlin for her editorial input.

The Crafty Leprechaun is a tale that has been passed down through the years.

Contents

Benny the Bed   1
The Crafty Leprechaun   21
Snow White's Revenge   33
Johnny Trumpy Bottom   55
The giant who loved to dance   66
Princess for a Day   77
Laddie, the little street dog   100
Adventures in Time   110
A bird in the hand   126
The great Fairy rescue   139

Once upon a time ….

Benny the Bed

In a little town, not so very far away, at the bottom of a hill, there sits a junkyard. In the middle of the junkyard sat a little wooden wonky house, no bigger than a shed and in this small, cosy home lived Bertha, a cuddly old woman who looked after the yard.

Bertha had a little nose, a crinkly face, wore thick black glasses and was always cheerful and smiley. People would bring their unwanted things to the junkyard and give them to the old woman. If it wasn't too shabby, she would clean them up and place them somewhere in the yard, but if it was unusable, she would cart it off to be crushed in a big crusher.

Bertha had a little dog – a pug called Cupid, who was as old as she was and on warm evenings, they would sit with the door of the house open. She would dunk biscuits into her mug of tea and the old dog would sleep on her knee, as she watched the stars.

But one day, Bertha received a letter inviting her to the Junkyard of the Year ceremony. The junkyard had been nominated and she was so chuffed, that she looked in the rails of discarded dresses and picked out one that she liked best.

She gave Cupid an extra dog biscuit and after a long goodnight cuddle, she jumped onto her bike and cycled off to enjoy the evening. The bicycle was far too tall for her and she wobbled back and forth along the road. As she peddled away, she never saw the two good-for-nothing thieves waiting in their van parked nearby.

Known as the Fibberscuttle brothers, or sometimes as the Bogey Brothers, Jake and Jimmy laughed through their dribbly noses as they watched the old woman go.

"There she goes! The place is ours!" giggled Jake.

"When the cat's away, the dogs can play!" added Jimmy.

"Don't you mean when the cat's away, the mice can play!" corrected Jake. Jimmy was always getting things topsy-turvy.

"Don't be such a numbskull. The dogs would chase the mice away!" Jimmy replied.

When they were sure she could no longer see them, they drove over to the entrance. It didn't take long for Jake to break the lock on the gate and they drove in and parked their noisy, smoke-belching van in the middle of the junkyard.

The old dog heard the engine, but curled up in her bed in the corner and returned to her dream of chasing rabbits.

"Might find some thing-a-ma-jigs here worth somefink, eh?" whispered Jake, wiping his long pointy nose and looking around at the walls of unwanted things piled up on all sides of the yard.

The two brothers were not very clever and wouldn't know if something was worth a million pounds or ten pence.

"Let's get started!" replied his brother Jimmy.

They poked into the corners and under old mattresses and found things they thought they could sell on to someone else. They threw them into the back of their van, rubbing their hands greedily, imagining piles of cash as they did so.

Finally, they walked to the little wonky house in the middle of the junkyard and peered in through the window.

"E-er, look!" cooed Jake. "Do you see that bed?"

"Yeah, 'course I see it, I'm not deaf!" replied Jimmy.

"Well" explained Jake, his eyes dancing in his head, "It's mum's birthday tomorrow. She'd love an old bed like that!"

Jimmy's face lit up.

"Hey! I've got an idea!" Jimmy announced.

"Wot?" replied Jake.

"You know what day tomorrow is?"

"Sunday?" replied Jake, a little unsure.

"No, you twonk! It's mum's birthday!" replied Jimmy!

"Yeah!" said Jake, excitedly.

"And you know what that means, don't you?" asked Jimmy.

"Cake!" replied Jake, hopping up and down, like on over-excited loon.

"Apart from cake!" groaned Jimmy, rolling his eyes. "We have to get her a present! Well, I fink she'd love an old metal bed like that one!"

Jake looked at his brother, confused.

"Didn't I just say that?" he asked.

"Well, if you did, I fink I would have heard you say it, I'm not completely blind, yer know!" replied Jimmy and opened the door to the little wonky house.

They tip-toed in and seeing the sleeping old dog, silently picked up the bed and carried it out and threw it into the back of their van and quickly drove off.

They laughed and gave themselves a pat on the back as they

trundled off down the road. They were so pleased with themselves. They laughed so hard in fact, that their noses dribbled even more so than normally.

"Hey, stinky-breath, have you done a poo?"

The brothers looked at each other.

"Hey, Jimmy, that's not very nice!" said Jake, offended by the allegation.

"I didn't say it!" replied Jimmy.

"Whooo, what a stink!"

They stopped the van with a screech and jumped out.

"Someone must be hiding in the back of the van!" Jake's voice trembled.

"Okay, okay!" replied Jimmy, pretending to be brave. "Don't get into a flapdoodle over it!"

They slithered along the outside of the van and after counting to three, they opened the back doors. Using a flashlight, they peered in. The things they had stolen were all they could see. No one was in the van. They scratched their heads and picked their noses, but they couldn't figure out where the voice had come from. They decided that it must have been voices on the radio and they jumped back in and drove quickly to their mum's.

When they arrived at her house, they unloaded the metal bed and carried it up to the front door and rang the bell. When old Ma Fibberscuttle opened the door, she was very surprised to see them and even more surprised and delighted with her birthday present.

They carried it into her bedroom and removed the old bed and put the new stolen one in its place.

"Happy Birthday, mum!" they both said and started singing the "Happy-Birthday-to-you" song – very badly.

They were terrible singers. If there was a prize for the worst singers in the world, the Bogey Brothers would definitely win.

"Ooooh, no! STOP!!" shouted their mother and rushed them out of the house, slamming the door after them.

Even so, as they drove off, they were feeling very proud of themselves.

But their happiness was short-lived, for the very next morning, their telephone rang and it was their mum, who was far from happy.

"I've had a terrible night's sleep. It's that bed, there's something wrong with it. It kept making farty sounds!"

"Now, mum, are you sure it was the bed?" replied Jimmy.

"It kept calling me names!" his mother insisted.

"What did?" Jimmy was confused.

To be fair, it didn't take much for Jimmy to be confused.

"The bed! Called me names and doing fart sounds." Ma Fibberscuttle shouted down the phone.

"Maybe you imagined it!" suggested Jimmy.

"Don't talk codswallop!" she replied. "I want it taken out of here and I want the old one back!"

"But, mum!"

"I want it taken away. I'm not having someone tell me I'm a smelly old fart bum! Especially if that someone is a bed!!!"

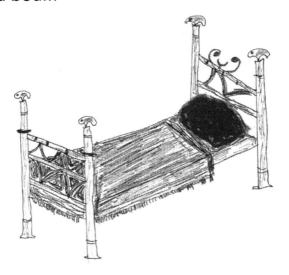

"She's gone doo-lally!" said Jake when he heard what his mum had said.

"Well, bonkers or not, she doesn't want the bed!" replied Jimmy.

They placed a "For Sale" advert in their local shop window straight away and that afternoon, the two brothers removed the old metal bed from their mother's house. They were so upset, because now they would have to find another present for her birthday. Fortunately, there was good news. They already had an offer on the bed.

They drove to a house not too far from the local shop and delivered the bed to its new owner and quickly made their escape.

However . . . the very next morning, their telephone rang again. This time, it was the man who had bought the bed. He was not very happy.

"That bed called me Knobbly Knees! And accused me of breaking wind. Which I did not!"

So, once again the two dribbly-nosed brothers, threw the bed into the back of the van. Jimmy almost cried when he had to hand the money back.

"What we going to do? Maybe we should just dump it?" suggested Jake.

"You know wot I fink?" asked Jimmy.

"Er ... no!" replied Jake, after a couple of minutes trying to read his brother's mind.

"I fink, we should just dump it!"

Jake was amazed.

"You must have read my mind, Jimmy. That's just wot I was finking too, as well!"

"Well, you know wot they say, little bruvver, two minds are better than one mind that isn't awake!"

And so, they dumped the bed onto the side of the road and drove off. As they did, they were sure they heard a voice shout "Windbag Pooey Bums!" at them. They pretended not to hear.

It wasn't long before someone came walking along the pavement. It was a little old man, who sadly was homeless. He had spent many nights sleeping on park benches and couldn't believe his luck when he saw a lovely, comfy-looking bed abandoned on the side of the road.

He wheeled it along until he found a narrow lane next to the local park. He pushed it against a wall, which had long, beautiful tree branches overhanging. He lay down on the bed. Oh how lovely it felt.

The sun was beginning to go down in the sky and a few stars were twinkling overhead. The old man closed his eyes and sighed and felt happiness the like of which he hadn't felt for years.

"Well, at least you don't smell too badly!"

The old man opened his eyes and looked around. He was sure he had heard a voice. But there was no one there.

"Hello?" he called.

"Do you snore?" the voice asked.

The old man was very confused. The voice sounded like it was right beside him. He quickly looked under the bed. No one was there.

"Who is speaking?"

"The name is Benny. Benny the bed!"

The bed gave a little shake and the old man realised that the voice was coming from the metal railings at the head of the bed.

"I must be dreaming!" said the little old man, scratching his head.

"Bit of a stupid dream! If it was a dream. Which it isn't." Benny the bed replied. "What's your name?"

"Er . . ." it had been so long since anyone had asked the old name his name, that for a moment he actually had forgotten it. "Robert!" he said at last.

"Well, I'm Benny! Benny the bed!"

"How can you talk?"

There was a pause and then Benny replied.

"Don't know!"

The old man was astonished. For the next few hours, he talked with Benny and learned all about him.

"Yes, I've had all sorts sleeping on me. But it gets a bit boring after a while. So, I decided to have a bit of fun. I started with just waiting until they were fast asleep and then I would make a big long fart noise!" Benny couldn't control his laughter.

"So, how come you ended up here?"

Benny told Robert all about how the two thieves had robbed the junkyard and taken the bed from the old woman's little wonky house. On hearing this, Robert stopped and thought for a moment. Then, he climbed off the mattress and took hold of the bed and dragged it back up the little lane.

When they arrived at the junkyard, the gate was still open and when he pushed the bed inside, Bertha appeared at her front door and smiled a huge smile. She was so delighted to have her old bed back again. She had missed the many, funny chats they'd had over the years.

Robert helped her put it into the ramshackle house and wished her goodnight. However, just before he had time to leave, Bertha stopped him.

"Wait. There's another old bed just came in this afternoon. It's just over there next to the pile of mattresses. You're welcome to come here every night and sleep, if you want!"

At last, Robert had found a home. Finally, he had something soft to sleep on. His own raggedly bed was placed under a battered, unwanted gazebo that they had put up next to the old wonky house and on warm mild evenings, Robert, Bertha, Cupid and Benny sat under the stars, dunking biscuits into mugs of tea and telling fart jokes.

The Crafty Leprechaun

This story was told to me by my father. His father told him. My great grandfather told my grandfather and someone even older than all of them told it to him. So, it's an old, old, old story. O. L. D. As old as a Leprechaun's beard, in fact. Which is very old.

It all happened one warm summer's evening, and the moon shined almost like the sun in the cloudless sky and Paddy Murray made his way back home, along the banks of the Boyne River in the county of Louth.

He was picking up stones and throwing them into the water of the river, which flowed like a sheet of glass and the plop of the stones as they hit the surface was the only sound to be heard. That is, until Paddy heard another sound, coming from a field behind a hedge running alongside the narrow path.

It was the sound of a small voice singing. Paddy stepped over and pushed quietly through the hedge and there beyond, in a field of rose bushes, sat a little Leprechaun.

Paddy couldn't believe his eyes. He had heard about the little people all his life, but never had he laid eyes on one.

The old stories were right though; the Leprechaun was indeed about three feet in height, dressed in a green jacket, brown trousers, shiny buckles on his shoes and a battered top hat. He also knew from the stories that a Leprechaun had a pot of gold hidden away somewhere and if you were lucky enough to get hold of one, he had to give his gold to you.

Well, Paddy moved slowly through the bush, never looking away from the little man singing to himself as he cobbled together a pair of shoes. For the Leprechauns loved to make shoes.

Paddy crept like a lion sneaking up on his dinner. Had the Leprechaun at any moment looked up from his work, surely he would have seen Paddy Murray come toward him. The moon was like a light bulb in the sky, so that nothing could remain hidden. But the little man didn't look up and before he knew it, Paddy grabbed hold of him by the collar of his green jacket.

Oh, how the Leprechaun squealed with the shock.

"I got you!" says Paddy, roaring with laughter, delighted with himself.

"Let me go! Let me go!" cried the Leprechaun, his tiny eyes staring up, terrified.

"I will not", says Paddy! "Do you think I'm a fool? I've caught you, so I want the pot of gold!"

"What pot of gold?" asks the Leprechaun. "I've no gold. I'm down on me luck, so I am! Gold! That's a good one. Sure, if I had gold, would I be sitting here making meself a pair of shoes? No! I'd be out buying shoes, wouldn't I?"

"Don't be trying that", says Paddy, "Everyone knows that if you catch a Leprechaun, they have to lead you to their pot of gold"!

"Leprechaun? Is it bonkers you are? I'm not a Leprechaun!" he says, "I'm just a little school-boy!"

"No, you're not!" says Paddy, "Whoever heard of a school-boy with a beard?"

And sure enough, the Leprechaun had a lovely red beard.

"Ah, alright, so, you've caught me. But what would you want gold for? Wouldn't you rather I gave you the gift of always being happy instead?" says the Leprechaun.

Paddy laughed so hard, he almost let go of the Leprechaun's collar.

"Don't you worry, I'll be happy enough with the gold!" replied Paddy.

The Leprechaun knew he wouldn't be able to talk the greedy man out of it, so he pointed to the rose bush he'd been sitting at.

"It's down under that bush!" he says "About three feet under there!"

Now, Paddy thought for a minute. He'd need to go home and return with his shovel and he remembered that once a Leprechaun gives his word, he would never break it. He reached into his pocket and took out his handkerchief. It was white with red dots on it.

"Now", says Paddy, "You must give me your word! The gold is under this bush here, you say?"

"It is!" replied the Leprechaun.

"Well, I have to go home and get me shovel to dig with and I'm going to tie my hankie around this bush. You must promise not to remove it. You must give me your word, you won't take my hankie off this bush!"

The little Leprechaun smiled and his eyes twinkled in the moonlight, like a baby laughing for the first time.

"I give you my word!" he replied. "I won't take your hankie off this bush! I won't!"

That was good enough for Paddy. He tied the handkerchief around the rose bush, laughing as he did so and then he was off like a mad man. He bolted through the hedge and onto the pathway again, next to the river. He lived a mile or two further along in a little place called Tully-allen.

He ran like his feet were on fire. He burst into his shed and grabbed his shovel and without stopping for breath, he ran back to the field of rose bushes.

As he got nearer, he couldn't stop laughing. He whooped and hollered and almost did a cartwheel, he was so excited. He'd be the richest man in the county when he got that pot of gold.

He thought of all the things he was going to be able to buy and got so excited, he almost fainted at the idea of it all.

At last, he spotted the gap he'd made in the hedge and he ran a little quicker and burst through into the field. Paddy's smile dropped and his eyes bulged out of his head.

The Leprechaun was nowhere to be seen, but he hadn't broken his promise. He had given his word and he hadn't removed Paddy's handkerchief. But on every rose bush in that very large field, there was an identical white handkerchief, all with red dots on them, just like Paddy's.

With the help of the bright moon, he could see that the field must have held a thousand rose bushes and each one had a handkerchief tied around it.

But Paddy wasn't going to give up that easily. He started digging. He uprooted one rose bush after another. He dug until his hands ached and swelled up. But he didn't stop. He tore up rose bush after rose bush until finally, the moon had faded and the morning sun was peeping up to say hello. By now, only two rose bushes were left standing.

Paddy pushed the shovel into the ground and heard a roar. Across the field, coming through the gate, his face full of anger ran Jack Cleery, the farmer who's field Paddy had destroyed.

"What are you doing to me roses?" he screamed, as he trampled across the field.

Paddy thought about trying to talk to Farmer Cleery, to tell him about the Leprechaun and the gold. But when he saw how angry he was and the size of the stick he had in his hand, he decided he wouldn't. He turned and ran. He was delirious with tiredness and the furious farmer had long legs and soon caught up with him.

"Come here and I'll flatten you!" the farmer shouted.

Paddy stumbled through the hedge and as he did, the large foot of the farmer kicked him in the bottom. It was a powerful kick and Paddy went flying.

He went about five feet into the air and landed in the river, with a great big splash. The farmer stood on the pathway, calling at him in Irish, threatening all sorts. Paddy kicked and swam like his life depended on it. He didn't look back and kept swimming until he reached the Irish Sea, and for all anyone knows, he hasn't stopped swimming yet.

Snow White's Revenge

Snow White was a beautiful young girl. In fact, she was as nosey as she was beautiful and as we already know ... she was beautiful. She lived in a wonderful castle.

But of all the rooms, in the castle, she had always wondered what her step-mother's bed chamber looked like and one afternoon, when she was fairly certain she wouldn't be caught, she crept along the castle corridors and entered the Queen's private room.

It was a stunning room. The bed was HUGE! You could have had twelve life-sized cuddly elephant toys in the bed and still have room to spread out. Next to the bed, on a little raised altar, was the Queen's dressing table. Above the table was a large mirror. It was as tall as Snow White and had a gold frame, with swirly edges.

She had heard the servants whisper about a Magic Mirror that told you everything you'd need to know. Perhaps the rumours were true. She decided to try it out for herself. She stood in front of the mirror and looked at her own reflection.

"Er ... hi!" she said, feeling a bit silly.

The mirror remained silent.

"Hey?" she called, but again the mirror gave no reply. She was getting annoyed now at being ignored.

"Oi! Are you a magic mirror or not?"

Her reflection in the mirror disappeared and little wispy clouds started to appear instead. The clouds billowed and broke apart and finally formed a face.

"I am!" replied the cloudy-face in the mirror.

"Oh! What's your name?" She asked.

"I have been called many things. Great Mirror. Wonderful Mirror. Brilliant Mirror! Fabulous Mirror!"

"Alright! A bit full of yourself!" Snow White commented.

"Most people just call me 'Magic Mirror'!"

"Oh, okay. So, Magic Mirror … er, do I have black hair?"

The cloud-face stared back at her for a moment and then sighed.

"Well … duh!" the mirror finally replied.

This was obviously a cheeky mirror and Snow White was a bit offended.

"Okay, what's the capital of France?"

The magic mirror's cloud-face swirled and a picture of a city appeared.

"The city you seek is Paris!"

Snow White gave a little squeal of delight. She jumped up and down and clapped, excited to ask another question.

"Magic Mirror … Am I beautiful?"

"Beauty you have. Beautiful you are. So .. er . . . yeah!" the mirror replied, to which Snow White was thrilled and gave a little curtsey.

"Am I the most beautiful in the land?"

The swirls of cloud moved in circles in the mirror.

"Beautiful indeed you are. But there is one more beautiful than you."

Snow White was a little hurt and started to feel heat in her cheeks.

"Who?" she demanded.

The cloudy swirls moved and formed a face. Snow White couldn't believe it.

"The Queen."

"My step-mother? Yuck! No way! Her nose is crooked! Silly mirror!"

The jealous Princess turned and stormed out of the room. She marched straight up to her own bedroom and sat down and stared out of the window. She knew what must be done. She must get rid of the Queen!

Now, it so just happened that Snow White had heard of a witch that lived in the forest and so she set off to find her.

As she walked through the woods, she came across an apple tree. She reached up and plucked a nice juicy red one off the branch and began to form a plan in her mind.

She would get the witch to make a poison and dip the apple into the poison and give it to her stepmother to eat.

She was so pleased with her plan, she whooped for joy. It was then that she noticed a small wooden house next to a stream. She thought to herself that this must be the home of the witch and so she ran across the grass and pushed open the door. Inside, she was quite surprised how small the place was. Her head was almost at the ceiling. There was a long table with seven little wooden chairs and seven tin plates set for dinner. Over the fireplace she noticed a framed photo of seven strange little men, sitting on a boat on a lake inside a cave.

"Hey!" a tiny voice called.

Snow White turned to see a pile of little men tumble through the front door. They seemed quite annoyed at her presence.

"Who are you?" demanded one, furiously.

"What are you doing in our house?" called another, stomping his little foot on the floor.

"And most importantly," asked another, "Did you bring lollipops?"

"No, why would I? she replied.

"Any polite person visiting someone would bring lollipops!" the little man informed her.

The other men fully agreed and told her so.

"But I didn't come to visit you!" the Princess replied. "I'm Snow White!" I'm looking for a witch!"

The men all called at once for the girl to leave their house, as they'd had a long day at the cave and needed to eat. The princess was not pleased with how she had been spoken to, but was in a hurry and didn't stay to put them in their place.

Soon, she could see a light glowing from the small round windows of another little cottage. Smoke was billowing from the crooked chimney on the roof and as she approached, she could hear singing coming from inside.

When she reached the front door,
she didn't knock, but instead just pulled
down the handle and stepped inside.

"Hello!" she called and the
singing stopped.

The room was filled with all sorts
of furniture. Armchairs, sofas,
footstools and tables, all cluttered with
books and bottles and bowls and

cakes. There was a large fireplace, with a huge cauldron over it, with something bubbling inside and the room was lit with candles everywhere. On every shelf, birds were perched with their eyes staring back at the princess.

"Hello?"

Snow White looked around and couldn't see anyone who may have been singing and she wondered that maybe one of the birds had been trained to sing. Then, she noticed a huge plume of hair nesting on top of a little wrinkled face, poking out from behind a large armchair.

"Hello, I didn't mean to disturb you!"

"What do you want?" asked the little woman in a croaky voice, as she came waddling out from behind the chair and shuffled over to the princess.

She was a tiny woman, with tiny eyes, but with a nose that looked like a sausage, which made her eyes look even smaller. Snow White noticed another face look at her. It was a cat, which was sat on top of the witch's head, wrapped up in the old woman's hair.

"Are you a witch?"

The old woman cackled and snorted with laughter and fell onto a nearby sofa. The princess was a little annoyed at being laughed at. She didn't see how it was funny and told the old woman so.

"You're absolutely right!" the witch replied. "It's not funny at all!"

"Then, why did you laugh?"

The old woman thought for a moment and then laughed even louder.

"I don't know!" she replied, rolling onto her side.

"I need to talk to you!" scolded Snow White.

The witch sat upright and held up her hand and a cup of tea appeared out of nowhere. She sipped from the cup and listened.

"What can I do for you?"

Snow White told the old woman everything. About how she wanted to be the most beautiful and how the mirror had told her that the Queen was! When she finished, she held up the apple she had taken from the tree and the old woman jumped off the seat and grabbed the fruit.

"I don't normally do harmful spells!"

"Well, can you do it or not?" demanded Snow White and the old woman's face creased in a big smile as big as her face and she hopped over to a nearby shelf and grabbed an armful of bottles, all with different coloured liquids inside them.

She set to work and finally dipped the apple into the devilish brew. At last, she scooped the apple up, dabbed it dry and handed it back to the girl.

"There! Now listen, this is my first time doing a horrible spell. So, even though the poison will work immediately, if you change your mind and wish to save the Queen …"

Snow White put the apple into her apron pocket and turned and skipped to the door.

"Don't worry, I won't!"

As she walked down the corridor to her stepmother's chamber, she felt nervous and also a little excited. She held the poisoned apple and hoped it didn't slip out of her hand.

She knocked on the door and stepped inside. The Queen sat at her mirror, brushing her long hair and seeing her like this made Snow White feel more determined than ever.

"Hello, my dear, did you have a good day?"

"Yes, stepmother. I went for a walk in the woods! I picked you something!"

Snow White held out the juicy red apple and the Queen's face brightened with joy. She took the apple and pulled her step daughter into her arms and gave her a warm hug.

"Thank you, my sweet girl! I'll have it later!"

The Queen placed the apple on the dressing table and Snow White waved goodbye and walked toward the door. She glanced behind and saw that the Queen had turned back to the mirror.

Snow White pretended to leave. She quietly crept across the room and very carefully slid herself behind a long curtain nearby. She wanted to watch the Queen eat the apple.

She peered through a gap in the curtains and saw her stepmother pick up the apple and hold it in her hand. She seemed to be looking at it, deciding which side to bite into first. Suddenly the door opened and her father, the King walked in.

"Ah, my darling!"

The King and Queen embraced and Snow White rolled her eyes at them.

"What's this?" asked the King, gesturing to the apple in his wife's hand.

"Oh, you'll never guess! Snow White brought it for me, as a gift!"

"Oh how sweet!"

"I know!" replied the Queen. "I didn't have the heart to tell her that I was allergic to apples and couldn't eat it!"

"Don't worry," replied the King, taking the apple, "I'll eat it!"

With that, he took a big bite from the fruit. Snow White felt her heart jump in her chest.

"No!" she screamed and ran out from behind the curtain.

Her parents looked at her, confused, but before they could ask her what she had been doing hiding behind the curtain, the King felt a pain in his body like never before.

He gasped for air and fell to the floor.

"Daddy!" cried Snow White, running to her father's side.

In the next few minutes, the room was filled with shouts and screams and tears. Doctors came, but no one could understand what was happening to their beloved King. He was still breathing, but he could not be woken and his heartbeat was slower and beating less often with each passing minute.

Finally Snow White admitted what she had done. She felt so ashamed. After she had told all, her stepmother gently lifted her face to hers and with tears in her eyes, told Snow White that it was alright and that she forgave her.

"Beauty is in the eyes of the beholder" she told her.

The Queen ordered all the staff out of the room and went and stood in front of the magic mirror.

"Mirror!"

"Yes, my Queen?"

The Queen's reflection faded and the misty face appeared instead.

"How can we save the King?"

"Poisoned he is. Poison from a witch's brew. But if he drinks from the enchanted lake . . . The spell of death will soon undo!"

"Where is this lake?"

"The lake is known to only the little men!"

Snow White knew what needed to be done. She ran from the room and along with ten of the best horsemen in the kingdom, they rode through the woods and arrived back at the house of the seven little men.

She opened the door and immediately was met with a cry of annoyance from the grumpy bunch, who were sat at the table eating their dinner.

"Here she is again!" cried one.

"Have you no manners?" asked another, slamming his fist on the table.

"And another thing!" demanded one, "Have you brought lollipops?"

Snow White grabbed the photo off the mantelpiece.

"The lake in this picture! Where is this lake?"

Snow White quickly explained what had happened. The men agreed to take her to the lake, which was in a cave near to their cottage and after she had filled a bottle with the cold water, she rode back to the castle.

It didn't take long for the water to do its magic and the King sat up from his strange, enchanted sleep.

From that moment onward, no one ever asked the opinion of the mirror, ever again.

Johnny Trumpy Bottom

Johnny Hardy was a small boy with a big problem. He always played on his own. That wasn't the problem. He didn't mind playing on his own. Mostly, he was a happy little fella. Always smiling and laughing and had so many imaginary friends, he sometimes couldn't decide which one was his best friend. You see, Johnny's problem was he couldn't stop breaking wind.

Even as a baby, he would fart almost all the time. Normally, when a baby is born, the first sound they make is a cry. Johnny's first sound was PPPLUUUT! He farted so loudly that the nurses thought that he had exploded.

All the time, as he grew up, awake or asleep, he would fart. To Johnny, it was just the same as yawning, hiccupping, sneezing or even breathing. It got to the point, that he stopped noticing. But when he started school, the other kids definitely noticed.

At first they laughed. Fortunately, the sound wasn't followed by a stinky smell. But even so, the kids pretended they could smell something. They would laugh, hold their noses and run away from him.

After a while, Johnny stopped chasing after them. Because when he did, he just farted again and they'd run off, laughing even harder.

It was impossible to play hide and seek with him. If he was hiding, you could always find him, because his bottom whistles gave him away. If he was the seeker, you always knew when he was near, and so you could easily creep away and find another hiding place.

They had many nicknames for him; Johnny Fart Bum, Sir Farts-a-lot, Whoopee Cushion, Hardy Farty, Johnny Trumper, Stinky Bottom, Balloon Bum and finally Johnny

Trumpy Bottom. This is the one that stuck.

It became so acceptable to call him Johnny Trumpy Bottom, that once during register, even his teacher - Miss Custard called him Johnny Trumpy Bottom by mistake.

There were other children who came along and had other disgusting habits and unfortunate problems. For a short time, they drew everyone else's attention away from Johnny. There was Dribbly Nose Nancy, Bogie Eater Barry, Vomiting Violet, Wee-wee William and Burpy Ben.

There were even a few teachers with habits and problems that made the children giggle behind their backs. There was Mister Peachy, who was bald, but wore big curly wigs that were far too big for his head.

There was Miss Kent, who had terribly smelly arm pits and then there were Miss Leach and Mister Cook, who obviously liked each other, but went bright red and couldn't speak whenever they were near one another. But all these were nothing compared to Johnny's farts.

Maybe because, as well as their volume and frequency, there was a wide variety of them. There were ones that sounded like a duck quacking, some like a balloon popping, or a whistle tooting. Some trailed off, some spluttered like a car engine trying to start. You knew one was coming, but you never knew what it was going to sound like.

With a little bit of practice, Johnny realised he could make his farts sound any way he wanted. This gave him a lot of enjoyment. He would sometimes sit by the front door and wait for the postman to push a parcel through the letter box and he would fart like the sound of a dog barking. He would roar with laughter when he heard the postman run away from the door.

He used to prank his mum and dad, by farting like the sound of the telephone ringing.

And in school, he would let one go and made it sound like a cat's meow and watch the teacher search the classroom for a stray cat.

It got so bad, that the head teacher, Miss Hinkenlooper, called Johnny's mum and dad into the school. She wanted to discuss the possibility of removing Johnny from the school, because the other students were too distracted by the sound.

Mrs Hardy was furious at the suggestion and wagged her finger at the thin, sharp-nosed head teacher.

"He can't help it!" said his mother, firmly. "It's a problem he was born with. And they don't smell!"

"But the noise!" pleaded the head teacher.

"If my son is asked to leave this school!" replied Johnny's mother, "I shall go to the newspapers and tell them that he is being discriminated against. By you!"

The thought of having her face splashed across the pages in the local newspapers, terrified the head teacher. So much so, that she let out a fart of her own, which was beyond her control.

It was agreed Johnny would be allowed to continue going to the school and given a seat blocked off from the other students in the class room. After some years, the other kids got used to the sounds of him breaking wind. It was almost as if he and his PPPHHUUUTT sound were invisible.

For a long time, things just carried on that way, until the day came when a poster went up on the notice board, announcing the school talent show.

Everyone was very excited about this. Lots of people put their name down to enter. Jilly Martin entered. She was a very talented dancer and was convinced she would win. Gary Palmer entered. He was given a magic set for Christmas two years ago and was sure he would definitely win. A few kids formed a gymnastics group. It seemed everyone had entered. And Johnny entered.

But when he was asked what his talent would be, he didn't answer. For the weeks leading up the show itself, Johnny practiced every minute he could.

Finally the big day of the talent show came. It was held in the main hall and all the parents were invited to attend. The place was packed. Everyone cheered and supported each contestant and then it was Johnny's turn. No one knew what to expect and some wondered if he could manage to get through it without letting a big stinker off.

Johnny took to the stage and for the next five minutes everyone watched, amazed at what they were hearing. You see, Johnny had managed to train his farts to sound like musical instruments. He had done such a good job of this that he was able to fart a song.

It sounded as if he had an orchestra in his underwear. He stood on the stage and his bottom played "Happy Birthday to me", "Jingle Bells" and to finish with – a medley of songs he had heard on television.

When he finished, there was a moment when Johnny faced the

audience and he wondered if he would be expelled from the school, but just as he took a bow, the place erupted in the biggest cheer and the loudest round of applause of the evening.

It was a decision everyone agreed upon – Johnny won the talent show and from then on, everyone in the school wanted to be seen with him. Some had even tried to copy his talent. Not too successfully though. Miss Hinkenlooper changed her tune too. She even asked Johnny to give extra music lessons to those in need. His talent was soon discovered elsewhere and he recorded an album. It was a two disc CD called "Now that's what I call farts"!

The Giant who Loved to Dance

Deep, deep down under the dark, dank earth, in Underworld, lived the giants.

It was a huge world, filled with rivers, mountains and lakes. There were volcanoes, bubbling with lava. Long tunnels wormed here, there and everywhere, leading to different parts of the underground universe. The giants lived in caves and holes in the earth's surface gave them sunlight. But mostly it was dark and hot and a little bit smelly. Maybe because of this, there wasn't a lot of laughter. No one sang, or painted pictures and no one had even heard of dancing.

Until Humphrey Bumblebung got bored one evening and left his cave and climbed up one of the tunnels, leading to the top of a tall mountain up above in Overland, which is what they called earth.

As he crawled out of the hole in the mountain, the cold air of Overland wrapped around his body and it felt wonderful. The stars sparkled in the sky. They looked like little dots of happiness and they made Humphrey smile. Then he looked down across the land to see lights twinkling from a tiny village.

He was always curious about the tiddly people who lived in Overland. They had a lot of strange and funny habits and he always returned to tell his fellow giants all about them. But they never seemed that bothered.

He trod as delicately as he could down the mountainside and across the fields and finally he towered over the village. There weren't any of the little creatures roaming about, but he could hear a strange sound coming from a large red-bricked building.

He lay on his belly and scootered closer. Over the door of the red-bricked building was a sign that read "Village Hall. Miss Hooper's Dance Club". There were large windows and Humphrey eased his face nearer and peered inside.

He couldn't believe what he was seeing. The little people were moving about in a bizarre manner. Sometimes, they held hands, sometimes they turned themselves in circles and Humphrey looked on and realised that they were moving in time with the strange sound. The sound stopped and the people clapped.

"Let the music continue!" called one of the little people inside and another sound started and the people started moving about again.

Humphrey realised that the sound he was hearing must be "music!" He looked back at the sign across the door and wondered, if this was what they called Dance!

When he returned to Underworld, he told anyone who would listen about what he had seen, but no one cared. When he did a demonstration of the dance, they looked at him like he had two heads. Even Penelope and Philippa Chugalunk, the two-head giant looked at him like that, which Humphrey thought was a bit two faced.

They mocked and jeered at him. He felt so small and so he didn't mention it again. Now and then, one of the giants asked him if he wanted to dance and then they would snicker at him and so he started to pretend he had just made the whole thing up. He couldn't understand why they all found it so odd. Whenever they mentioned it to him, he denied he liked dancing at all. It was a lie which made him so sad inside.

He tried to put it out of his mind completely. But Humphrey couldn't get rid of a strange feeling of emptiness in his stomach. He felt such joy watching the people dancing and wanted to do it himself and so, he began to creep away again. He would climb up onto the surface, find a deserted place and dance, all by himself.

Oh, how he loved to dance. He didn't know if he was a good dancer.

He didn't care. He just felt so good when he was doing it. Being good at it could come with practice. But, it made him so happy. Happier than when he ate ice cream with chocolate sprinkles! And ice cream with chocolate sprinkles was his favourite thing to eat in the whole world. So, now you get some idea of how happy it made him to dance. It was like Christmas and his birthday all rolled into one.

He secretly watched Miss Hooper's Dance Club every week and learned all sorts of dancing. He loved them all. He loved to jive, he loved doing the boogie woogie, the jitterbug, and something he made up himself which included spinning in a circle and waving his arms up and down like a flapping bird. He called it The Flappy Wavy Spinning Thing.

But the problem was – being a giant – Humphrey wasn't very light on his feet. When he danced, he would jump up and down, waving his arms, wiggling his bottom and feeling so happy. This made him dance even faster and when he danced even faster, the land about him rattled and the people in the little houses hid under their beds, because they thought there was an earthquake.

It was several weeks later, as Humphrey was creeping toward the village, when he felt a strange sensation that he was being watched. He stopped and stood still, pretending to be a tree. But he couldn't see anyone near the village. Then he realised there was someone behind him.

He turned to see Jennifer Jinkledink.

"What you doing following I?" he asked her.

"I'se want to see dancey people!" she replied and Humphrey knew she wasn't there to make fun of him.

The two giants eased across the field and on their tummies, watched the dancing couples in the village hall. Humphrey glanced to Jennifer and saw that sense of wonder in her face and knew she felt as he did.

"They calls that music!" he told her.

She didn't reply. She was too enchanted by it all.

Each night after that, more giants followed Humphrey and Jennifer up to Overland and their hearts melted as they watched the happy people dancing and as they shuffled back across the field, they wiggled their hips and jiggled their fingers to the beat in their feet.

Finally, one rainy-drenched night, a whole gaggle of giants left the mountain tunnel and stepped down the other side, away from the village and as the thunder rumbled and lightning cracked overhead, they danced with child-like joy.

As they made their way back to Underworld, they formed a conga line and danced all the way back. They didn't stop when they got back to Underworld. They danced until it was time to sleep. And some even danced in their dreams, as they slept.

Over time, more and more giants joined in and no one mocked any more. Dancing became part of the giant's way of life.

So, if one night, you hear a drumming and the windows rattle, it might be a storm . . . or it might just be some giants having a wonderful time, dancing.

Princess for the Day

The School bell clanged and the kids of Oakdeans walked quietly from their class rooms, hopping with excitement to reach outside. During the last hour, they had watched the snow fall heavily down in great big flakes and could hardly contain themselves.

The doors opened and outside had become a snow-filled wonderland. A waft of cold air whipped along the school corridor. Katie and her friends dashed out and immediately there was a snowball fight. There were several teachers in the playground at the time, but instead of calling for calm and making everyone drop their snowballs, they actually rolled up some snow and joined in.

After a while, Katie waved goodbye to her friends and skated across to the main gate. Out on the pavement, the snow scrunched under her feet and she loved the sound and so zig-zagged along on the way home.

The lights from the houses spilled onto the snowy streets, all in different colours. Christmas trees flashed in the windows and as Katie turned the key to her front door, she could smell something beautiful coming from the kitchen.

"I'm home!" she called and her mum called back at her from inside the kitchen.

As the front door shut, her dad entered the hall and gave her a hug.

"Good day at school?"

"It was alright!" shrugged Katie.

"Learn anything?"

"No, not really!" she replied.

"Great stuff! That's the last thing we'd want, eh!" her dad replied.

Her mum joined them in the hall.

"Right, upstairs!" her mum told her, "Go get dressed into something nice. We're going out!"

"Where?"

"It's a surprise!" replied her parents together.

As they walked down the street, the light in the sky had darkened. The snow was still falling and as they walked to the bus stop, the only sound they could hear was their shoes crunching down on the thick carpet of snow on the pavement.

"So, where are we going?" asked Katie again and again, but her parents just did one of those "you'll see faces" and smiled.

A bus and train ride later, they stepped onto a very busy platform. They rarely went into town and whenever they did, it was always busy. People going to work. People going home from work. And tourists. Lots and lots of tourists. But today was even busier. Christmas buzz was in the air as well as the falling snow.

As they walked out of the station, Christmas was all around them. There were market stalls and a colourful carousel, blinking Christmas lights and sounds of cars, street sellers and choirs singing Carols.

A man was selling roasted chestnuts from a metal barrel, with a fire burning underneath it and as they walked past, the smell was a mixture of chocolate and candyfloss. Katie imagined it was the same smell of Santa's beard.

"This way!" called her father and she held her parent's hands and they walked down a narrow street.

The shop windows were decorated with Christmas and fairy-tale scenes. Katie saw a beautiful red coat in one of the windows and told her father to "Keep that in your head!" which was her way of asking him to make a mental note for her Christmas list.

Dad nodded and smiled.

"I don't know if there's any more room in my head!"

They continued on down the street. Katie sensed her parent's excitement. Near the end of the road, they stopped and her dad pointed to the building opposite them. It was a theatre. Lights flashed over the doorway and Katie could see the poster of what show was being performed inside.

"Cinderella?"

Katie's heart jumped. She LOVED Cinderella. She had seen loads of Cinderella films and read tons of Cinderella books, each retelling the tale in different ways. Her favourite was the one when Cinderella becomes a pop star. She was Cinderella-mad! If there was a quiz on Cinderella, Katie was the expert.

"Come on, let's go!" her dad said and stepped off the kerb.

Katie felt she had been filled with pixie dust and they ran quickly across the narrow street and bounded up the steps and in through the wide theatre doors.

Inside was all reds, greens and every wall was filled with posters from old stage shows. The ceiling was a mirror and as her dad handed the attendant their tickets and her mum bought snacks and a programme, Katie looked around, dizzy with joy.

She tingled with excitement as they walked down the aisle toward the centre of the theatre, toward row F. They shuffled along until they reached their seats and sat down.

Immediately, the lights began to dim and music burst out over the loudspeakers. Katie noticed a little head moving about just in front of the stage. He waved his stick to the rhythm of the music.

"That's the conductor!" whispered her mum, clearly reading Katie's mind, as she was just wondering what the mad little fellow was up to.

"He's in charge of the music," added her dad. "He and the band are in the orchestra pit, which is in a big hole in front of the stage. The conductor tells them when to play!"

The velvety blue curtains rose and disappeared up into the ceiling over the stage. Katie gasped. The set was beautiful. It was a village market scene. Very similar to the beginning of Beauty and the Beast, thought Katie. And then, there she was – Cinderella. Dressed in rags, but glowing with beauty. Katie sank deeper in her chair, engrossed as the actors on stage played their roles just as she always imagined them.

The theatre filled with laughter at the funny parts and you could hear a few sniffles of sadness during the tearful moments. Katie sat forward. It was the scene when the horrible step-sisters had torn Cinderella's dress and left for the ball, laughing at their own bad behaviour.

You could have heard a pin drop in the theatre, as poor Cinders cried her heart out in the dusty kitchen, when the twinkling music started and flickering lights sparkled in the corner of the room.

Katie's heart was in her mouth. She knew what was going to happen next. The Fairy Godmother was about to appear. It was her second favourite part of the story. Her favourite part was when Cinderella goes to the ball dressed in the beautiful dress.

Cinderella stepped forward toward the front of the stage and there was a bright flash of smoke and the beautiful Fairy Godmother moved into the light. Shocked by the sudden appearance of the magical fairy, Cinderella turned quickly to see her. And what happened next made everyone in the audience gasp loudly.

As the actress playing Cinderella turned, her ankle twisted and she fell. Now if she had fallen onto the floor of the stage – that would been one thing. Embarrassing, maybe. Perhaps it would have made a few people chuckle. But the poor girl, fell backwards and down into the orchestra pit, with a great big bang. She had fallen past the conductor and landed on the drums, which caused a huge noise.

There followed a great kerfuffle. People ran up and down the aisles, the Fairy Godmother reached down into the orchestra pit, but was ushered away. Finally, the curtains came down and the lights went up.

Everyone in the audience started talking, all at once and Katie watched as several men in black T-shirts and wearing head-sets climbed down into the pit and after several minutes, the bruised face of Cinderella emerged. The audience cheered and clapped, as they watched her being helped up the steps onto the stage and disappear behind the curtain.

Katie was in a state of shock. She looked at her parents.

"This never happened in any of the other Cinderella stories I've read!"

Her parents laughed.

"It'll be okay" replied her father. "All these big shows have an understudy. So, if the actress playing the part gets ill, the understudy goes on and does the part!"

Katie was glad to hear it. She was so enjoying the show. The music was so beautiful, the sets were colourful, the lights made it all look so magical and she was desperate to see the ball room scene.

A few minutes passed. Nothing was happening. A few more minutes went by. Even more nothing was happening. Then the curtain began to move, as if someone was walking behind it. Suddenly, a man stepped out from the gap in the middle of the curtains and held a microphone to his mouth.

"Ladies and gentlemen!"

The noisy audience immediately became quiet.

"Ladies and gentlemen!" he repeated, "I'm very sorry for the interruption in the show. As you could see, our wonderful actress playing Cinderella had a nasty accident, but I can assure you, she is fine. No bones broken!"

The audience applauded.

"Phew!" added Katie.

"Now, usually under normal circumstances, the understudy would step in and the show would continue. However, I regret to say, our understudy is not here tonight, as she was taken sick with a tummy bug just this morning! And so . . . I am so very sorry, so extremely sorry, but the show cannot go on!"

There was a very loud groan from the audience, a few shouts of "What?" and "You are kidding me!" and Katie noticed a lot very cross faces.

"I paid good money to come here!" called out a very annoyed lady two seats in front of them.

"I'm sorry!" continued the little man on the stage, his voice now very shaky over the loudspeakers.

"Poor man!" said Katie to her mum, who nodded in sympathy.

"We simply can't go on . . . Unless . . .!" his voice trailed off. "Unless there's anyone in the audience that knows the story and doesn't mind coming up here and taking over!"

The audience mocked the suggestion. But, Katie turned to her parents. They leaned in to listen to her.

"I could do it", she whispered. "I could!"

"Well, that's the only thing I can think of!" said the man on the stage. "So, is there anyone who would like to volunteer?"

Katie put up her hand.

"Here!" called her parents, pointing at their daughter.

The audience were stunned into silence once more and turned to watch the little girl stand up.

"I can do it!" she said, in a small and slightly frightened voice.

"You? You can do it?" he called over the loudspeakers, sounding slightly hopeful.

"Yes!" replied Katie, a little louder and more confident.

"Oh, alright then. Make your way up here young lady!"

The audience roared. They cheered and clapped, a few laughed and shook their heads, but they all sat back down and Katie walked up the steps onto the stage to be met by the little man, who held open the curtain for her.

As soon as she stepped backstage, she was surrounded by

people. They were all so much taller than she was. They twittered like birds, talking so fast, so excited that Katie couldn't understand them.

Then, out of the crowd, a tall, slender woman breezed in calmly and looked down at Katie and smiled.

"Come with me!"

Katie was whisked away and in the next few minutes, she had people around her explaining what she needed to do. They asked her what songs she knew the words of. They showed her dance moves. They put dresses on her, then took them off her, then returned, with the dresses now fitting perfectly.

A young girl, who smiled so kindly, sat in front of her and started putting make-up on Katie's face.

"You're one of the step-sisters!" said Katie.

"That's me!"

"You are horrible!"

The actress burst with laughter.

"Thanks!"

"In a good way!" added Katie.

"Of course, sweetie!"

Soon, Katie was dressed as Cinderella.

She was taken and placed on a white dot painted on the middle of the floor. A few feet away, the curtain hung in front of her. She looked off into the sides of the stage and it was filled with people all giving her the thumbs up.

Katie took a deep breath. She didn't stop to think about what she had agreed to do. If she did, she probably would have run back to her parents.

The music started. It was too late to change her mind now. The curtain began to rise and suddenly Katie was blinded by the lights beaming at her on the stage. She could see the conductor in the pit in front of her, waving his stick and smiling like a mad man up at her, but when she looked out at the audience, she could hardly see a thing. However, she could hear them. They cheered for her.

Behind her, a flash of light burst across the stage. Katie – as Cinderella – spun around and there standing facing her was the Fairy Godmother.

"You shall go to the ball, my dear!" announced the Fairy Godmother and the audience whooped and cheered.

For the next hour, Katie played the part of Cinderella and loved every minute of it. Her favourite part was the ball room dance, of course, followed closely by the scene when she had to place her foot in the glass slipper.

As she took her bow, the whole audience stood up. They cheered, screamed, whistled and Katie swelled with pride. Especially so, when she saw her mum and dad standing on their chairs, waving up at her.

As they left the theatre, she stopped to sign autographs and pose for photos for so many people that they had to get two security men to stand with her. A star was born!

And as a special thank you, the theatre manager arraigned for a long-stretch limousine to drive her and her parents' home.

It was the best day ever!

Laddie, the Little Street Dog

Laddie was a small jack russell terrier. He had black and white hair, in a pattern that made him look like a tiny cow. He was a stray dog. He wasn't always a stray dog. However, he remembered the day when he became one very well. He'd never forget it. He had been brought for a car ride and then when the door opened and he had jumped out, the car had driven off without him.

For a time, Laddie sat on the pavement and waited. He couldn't understand why his master had not got out of the car when he did. Maybe he had forgotten something back at the house. And so, he waited. And waited. And waited some more.

But that was a long time ago now and his master's car never returned. Laddie had learned to live on the streets. He became very good at dodging cars, outrunning schoolboys and keeping away from foxes.

The streets could be a scary place. At first, he was very trusting of people. They came up to him and gave him a rub on his head, but then they grabbed him and tried to take him away. Laddie didn't like that and rolled and kicked and eventually he would get away from them. After a while, whenever he saw a person, he would find somewhere to hide from them.

When it rained, he would crawl under a parked car and lay down. But it was cold and smelly and sometimes the rain water crawled under him and it was very uncomfortable.

The hunger was the worst. Like every dog, Laddie loved his food. Finding something safe and tasty to eat was difficult.

He was always confused how the humans would throw food into bins and when he tried to get the food out of the bins, they would chase him away. Did they want it or not?

Humans were very confusing. They used to say "Who's a good dog?" Now, all they seemed to say was "Get away! Bad dog! Go!" They used to call him, "Pooch" or "Sweety", now they call him "Mutt!" Humans were crazy!

But in his dreams, they were so nice. Just like they used to be. Laddie dreamt a lot. Even when he wasn't asleep. He would daydream and sleep dream. His favourite dream was the

one he had about owning his own shop
– *Pedigree Pooches Pamper Parlour*!

It would be run by dogs for humans. He would have other dogs in charge of hair. Some would do nails. But he imagined himself trotting proudly through the shop. On either side, the humans would sit with their legs raised, smiling down at him as he went from one to the other, licking their toes!

But the toes in real life were in a boot or sharp shoe that always tried to kick him.

Because of how he was treated, Laddie started feeling differently about people. He started to growl at them if they came too close. He sometimes barked at them and when they had gone away, he felt so sad that he had done that. He didn't want to scare people. But he just didn't know what else to do.

One day, as he lay snoozling in an alleyway, next to a row of shops, he noticed a tiny, little girl playing with a doll. She seemed to be on her own. Laddie knew that wasn't good. He knew little children shouldn't be on their own outside shops and so he crept out and approached the squeaky child.

Keeping a good distance, he stood watching her.

She was a funny little creature, thought Laddie. She talked to her doll in one voice and then she would reply as the doll in another voice. Laddie wagged his tail. He wanted her to talk to him.

Suddenly, she walked off the pavement and crossed the road. Laddie barked, hoping someone would come and see the child. No one did. Laddie was delighted the girl got across the road safely. Luckily there were no cars speeding down the high street at the time.

But he did see the girl walking in the direction of the river. He barked louder. Inside the butcher shop, a woman turned and looked around. She ran out of the shop and seemed frightened.

Laddie barked up at her and ran out onto the road, wanting her to follow him. He looked back. The woman wasn't even watching him. He barked again and this time, the woman did see Laddie and also saw her daughter fall down the river bank.

Laddie ran. He was terrified for the little girl. He heard the mother shouting and she seemed to be terrified too. But when Laddie reached the place that the little girl had fallen from, he realised that she had rolled down the grassy bank and had gone straight into the river.

He dashed down the grass and without giving a second thought, dived into the icy water, with a great big splash. Laddie had never swam before and didn't even know if it was something he could do. As he paddled toward the little girl, he could hear her crying and saw that she was splashing and kicking and dipping under the surface. He realised, she couldn't swim.

The little girl went under the water and Laddie lunged down after her. His mouth made contact with her coat and he bit into it and held on and swam to the surface, kicking for all he was worth.

The woman reached down and grabbed her daughter and pulled her out of the river. Laddie found a shallow place that allowed him to jump up out of the water and he shook himself dry. He watched the woman hug and hold her daughter, who was coughing and more upset that she had lost her doll.

"Don't ever do that again!" cried the woman as she held her child.

Laddie noticed something on the river bank. He went and picked it up in his mouth. It was the doll. He padded over to the child and dropped it at her soaking feet.

She reached down and took it and then held out her hand to him.

Laddie inched forward and smelt the child's hand. He licked it and she giggled.

Little Laddie found a new family that day. The woman and her daughter brought him back to their house and from that day onwards, he had a warm bed, lots of food and tons of hugs and tickles. And as he lay, cuddled up in his basket, he had to admit – it certainly was a dog's life.

Adventures in Time

Every Summer, for as long as she could remember, Maggie and her family went to Norfolk. They always stayed in a really nice place that had areas for people to camp and other areas for caravans. They also had really big cabins that you could hire and they usually stayed in one of those. There was an indoor and outdoor pool on site and a shop and a restaurant.

Maggie quite liked it. She and her little brother, Daniel could go on their bikes, or go swimming or go fishing on a lake with their dad. There was even a steam train and they loved watching it roll by, big clouds of steam gushing out of its chimney. But once, just once, she wished they could go to Disneyland, or Spain or Greece on holiday.

But then one day something wonderful happened. Something, quite amazing.

Maggie and Daniel cycled from the cabin and peddled along the narrow pathways, through the woods. It wasn't long before they came across a tree with a rope hanging from a branch and they jumped off their bikes and took turns in swinging on the rope.

As Daniel jumped on for his turn, Maggie became aware of a strange whistling noise. She looked up into the overhanging treetops. They were shaking, as if ruffled by gusts of wind and suddenly something brushed through them. Maggie couldn't see what it was, but it was large and it parted the branches at the top of the trees and the whistling sound became a loud drone.

Suddenly, the object dropping from the sky flickered. Some moments it was visible, others it wasn't and it crashed into the middle of the field next to them.

Daniel joined his sister and they both watched in amazement at the large invisible object pressing down into the deep grass. Steam and smoke gushed out from the flattened blades of grass and then a loud electrical flash sent a wave of warm burnt air across their faces.

When the steam cleared, there in front of them, now visible was a large black object, in the shape of a pyramid. It was the size of a small house.

"Maggie, I'm scared!"

Maggie took her brothers hand and gave it a gentle squeeze.

"Don't be!" she replied.

As they watched the black pyramid, it started to flicker again and it slowly began to disappear completely. They waded across the tall grass and as they reached where they had seen the large object, they held out their hands and to their amazement, their fingers touched the thing.

"It's still here! It's invisible!"

As they walked around the object, a hissing sound erupted from one side and they froze in fear. They watched as a door slid across and from inside, four people stepped out. There was a man, a woman and two children, a boy and girl, both similar in age to Maggie and Daniel.

Daniel had learned about the Victorians at school before the summer holidays and he recognised the clothes these people were wearing.

"They're dressed like the Victorians!" he whispered to Maggie.

The four oddly dressed people emerged and as they stepped onto the field, the door glided back into place. They stared at the two children, who stared back at them.

"Hello, are you aliens?" asked Daniel, to which the four visitors glanced at one another and then began to laugh.

"What's so funny?" demanded Maggie.

"We're sorry" replied the lady, stepping closer. "We're not aliens. We're from Earth!"

The lady then explained that they were from the year 3030 and in the future time travel was possible and for summer holidays, instead of going somewhere, they went to some time.

People would go back to a particular time in history and mix in with the locals.

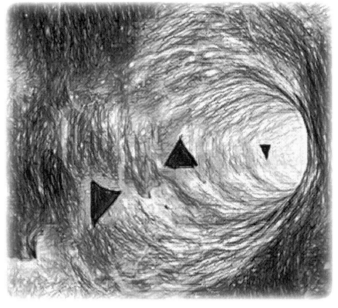

"Time travel?" repeated Daniel, excitedly.

"Yes. In the future, they discovered a time tunnel. There's pyramid shaped pods travelling through it all the time now!" explained the woman.

"Some people go to ancient Egypt, or Rome, Greece!" added the man.

"Yeah!" scowled the boy, "and if you have parents who aren't boring, you can even go back to the time of the dinosaurs!"

"Here we go again! Look, Toby, how many times are you going to complain about this? You know I'm allergic to dinosaur fur!"

"Oh, dad, you're allergic to everything!" replied the little girl.

"Jane, don't be rude to your father!"

"Sorry mum. Sorry dad!" replied Jane.

Maggie and Daniel listened as the visitors from the future argued about previous holidays.

"Why are you dressed in Victorian clothes?" interrupted Daniel.

"Well," replied the mother, "I've always wanted to go back to that time and just soak up the atmosphere!"

"But, this isn't Victorian times!" explained Maggie.

"Yes, we know!" replied the father. "There was a little malfunction! Our tour guide is inside working on repairing it!"

Just then, the door reopened and a small man, with a beard that almost reached his feet, stood in the opening.

"Good and bad news folks. I can repair the pod. Shouldn't take more than a couple of hours, but we will have to return to base!" he announced, to which the lady seemed very disappointed.

Maggie felt so sorry for the woman and an idea popped into her head. She whispered it to Daniel, who nodded in agreement.

It just so happened that very near where they were staying, there was an old Victorian museum that used to be a workhouse. They explained this to the time travelling tourists, who seemed to think it was a splendid idea.

"But how shall we get there?" asked Daniel, suddenly realising they would need transportation.

The little, long-bearded tour guide chuckled and a twinkle sparkled in his tiny eyes. He disappeared for a moment into the pod and returned, carrying six silver jackets.

"Here, put these on!" he said as he handed them out.

"What are they?" asked Maggie.

"You'll see!" he replied, adding "When you're ready, visualise this museum in your head".

When the jackets were on and buttoned, Maggie and Daniel started to picture the museum and suddenly they and the four visitors rose into the air. Then, they were off, flying high above the trees and zipping across the countryside below.

Very soon, the museum came into view and they slowly dropped to the ground nearby. They removed the jackets and hid them in a bush close to the entrance and went up to the main door.

Maggie and Daniel had visited this museum on many occasions. They played at being guides for the people from the future. There were workhouse bedrooms, a Victorian school, shops and a laundry.

The parents seemed to enjoy the experience, but Jane and Toby, who would rather be hiding from dinosaurs, shuffled along, obviously bored. This time, it was Daniel who had an idea.

After they had gone through the museum, they returned to the get their jackets and flew off to another attraction nearby.

As they landed, the two children from the future almost exploded with joy.

"Dinosaurs!" they exclaimed.

"What is this place?" asked the mother.

"It's Dino World. A dinosaur theme park!" replied Maggie.

"What's a theme park?" asked Jane.

"You'll see!" replied Daniel.

Indeed they did see. After they had rode on the T-Rex Rollercoaster, the Woolly Mammoth Log Flume and the Caveman Bone Crusher – which was a rollercoaster in the dark – they were theme park-mad!

When they arrived back in the field, the little long-bearded man was having a great time, cycling around on Maggie's bicycle. Even when he saw them returning and had climbed off the bike, he couldn't stop chuckling.

"I've read about these transportation devices, but that's the first time I've ridden one!" he giggled, hardly able to contain himself.

"Take it, you can have it!" replied Maggie. "I'll say I lost it!"

The little man was so touched by the gift, that he let them keep two of the silver jackets!

"I'll say I lost them!" he said and went inside the pod.

The four visitors were sad to leave. They all agreed that this had been the best vacation they'd had. Maggie and Daniel waved them goodbye, as the pod rose into the sky. With a gust of air, they catapulted upwards and disappeared beyond the clouds, with only a little puff of smoke left behind.

Maggie and her brother walked back to the cabin, reminding each other that it had all really happened. They could hardly believe it. But the two silver jackets were proof and when they arrived back, they hid the jackets in the shed behind the cabin, excited at the prospect of what adventures they would have tomorrow.

A Bird in the Hand

On her way home from school, one Friday afternoon, Molly saw something on the pavement next to her front gate. She stood over it and realised it was a small, baby bird. It was so tiny and squishy looking. It seemed like it had just hatched out of its egg, thought Molly. There was a tree nearby and she assumed it must have fallen out of its nest.

Luckily, it was still alive and Molly wondered how she could get the little creature back up into the branches. But then, she noticed the neighbour's cat come padding down the pavement toward her. She had no time to think, and so she gently and carefully scooped up the floppy bird into her hand and held it close to her.

126

She rang the doorbell and as soon as her mother opened the door, she dashed inside, leaving the curious, cat outside.

"What have you got there?"

"It's a baby bird!"

Molly showed her mum the delicate little thing.

"Poor little sausage!" whispered her mother and ushered Molly and the bird into the kitchen.

She watched her mum open the cupboard and take out one of her wooden salad bowls. Then taking a handful of cotton balls from another cupboard, she stretched them out into the bowl.

Molly gently placed the droopy bird in on top of the bed of cotton wool at the bottom of the bowl.

"What kind of bird is it, I wonder!" said her mother, to which Molly shrugged her shoulders.

"I'm going to call him Lucky!" said Molly and her mother smiled and nodded, agreeing that it was a great idea.

"Let's put him in the garden, in case its mother tries to find him!"

Molly followed her mum out into the back garden. She walked halfway down through the grass and over to the fence. It was covered with a thick growth of weeds, leaves and twisting bush branches growing through from next doors garden.

Her mother put her hand into the overgrown ivy and made a little hole and then they placed the wooden bowl into the newly formed cavity.

"There! That's a nice cosy place!" said her mother, to which Molly nodded happily.

They were about to go back inside, when something wonderful happened. An adult bird flew down out of nowhere and went straight into the hole in the hedge. Molly and her mum watched, not daring to make a sudden move.

Within a few minutes, the bird hopped out onto a branch, seemed to watch Molly for a moment and then flew off over the back wall.

Molly ran to the hedge and peered in. Lucky was still there, snuggled up in the cotton wool.

"Let's stay back!" whispered her mum and over the next hour, Molly watched bird after bird fly in, food in their beaks, visiting the wounded and hungry baby. Eventually, there was a long stretch of no visitors and Molly popped her head up to see the invalid. The baby chick was fast asleep.

The next morning, Molly looked out of her bedroom window into the garden below. She gasped. That cheeky cat from down the road was climbing onto the fence, heading toward the place where the baby bird was.

She ran downstairs and opened the back door and dashed outside. The cat was now on the grass and laying on her stomach, licking her lips. Molly's heart flip-flopped.

"Shoo!" she yelled and the cat, reluctantly slid off, acting as if she was the Queen of Cats.

Molly ran to the fence and looked into the hole in the hedge. All she could see was the bed of cotton wool. She felt her eyes begin to get wet and then something moved. Lucky popped his gangly head up out from under the cotton wool. He looked around and fell backwards.

"Phew. You are lucky!" she laughed and ran inside.

Grabbing the biggest spoon she could find, she filled it with some water from the taps. As she went back outside, she walked like she was a tightrope walker in a circus. She felt very proud that she hadn't spilled any of the water and she pushed it slowly through the opening.

Lucky took jerky little sips from out of the spoon and then fell backwards again onto the woolly bed.

"Maybe I should call you Clumsy"
Molly laughed.

For the next two weeks, more
and more birds – all different types of
birds – flew in to visit the baby in the
hedge and bring it food. Molly would
peer in and chatter to Lucky for hours
every day. The cat hadn't returned.

Each day, Lucky seemed to be getting bigger and bigger. He wasn't so floppy anymore and red feathers started to appear on his chest.

"Lucky is a robin red breast!" she told her mother.

Molly had noticed for a day or so, the birds in the area had stopped visiting the hole in the hedge. Then, one Saturday morning, as Molly opened the back door to visit her patient, she noticed a little robin red-breast, standing at the opening in the hedge.

The bird watched her as she stepped out of the house. Molly stopped.

"Hello, Mister Robin. How's our patient today?" she asked the little creature.

The robin moved its head to the side and gave a little tweet, as if to say "Doing nicely!"

"Oh, good" replied Molly, "Glad to hear that!"

The robin swooped across and landed on her shoulder. Now, their faces were so close to each other. Molly stared into the bird's eyes and at once felt that this was Lucky. All better and grown old enough to fly.

"Lucky? Is it really you?" she whispered.

The robin ruffled its feathers and whizzed off across the garden and disappeared over the back wall. Molly stepped forward and popped her head up and looked in. The wooden bowl was empty. Lucky had left the nest.

She waited and waited, but Lucky didn't return. Molly went inside and snuggled into her mother's arms, feeling like she had lost her best friend and then went upstairs to sit on her bed. She sat and held her favourite soft toy, Bubsey the Polar Bear.

Bubsey usually knew just the right thing to say to cheer her up, but today, he just looked back into her eyes, feeling a little sad himself.

Then Molly heard a sound. It seemed to be coming from outside her window. She stepped up and parted the curtains. The robin was stood on her window sill. Molly was so surprised. The bird chirruped and trilled and cocked its head back and forth.

Slowly, Molly opened the window and stood back. The robin flew in and landed on her bed, next to Bubsey, who wasn't a bit scared of the bird.

"Are you the baby bird?" asked Molly, "Are you my little Lucky?"

The robin gave a quick tweet and flew off the bed and landed on the shelf closer to Molly.

"You are, aren't you? I was so worried you'd never come back!"

The bird, hopped along the shelf. Molly held out her hand and was amazed when Lucky, the little robin hopped onto it. Molly wanted to shout down for her mum to come and see, but she didn't want to frighten the little bird.

Every day after that, Lucky would tap on Molly's bedroom window and pop in for a visit. He would sit as the little girl told him about her day and she would listen as he whistled and seemed to tell her all about his day. They were the best of friends.

The wooden bowl stayed wedged into the hedge growing over the fence and over the years, many birds laid their eggs on the soft cotton woollen bed that little Lucky had laid his floppy little head.

The Great Fairy Rescue

Lucy never dreamed she would ever meet a unicorn or fairy in real life. She had read stories about them, of course. But sometimes, the most magical things happen when you least expect it.

Her grandmother arranged for her to come and stay one weekend and on the first night, she snuggled down in the big, warm, cosy bed and soon she was fast asleep.

A noise woke her up. There was a gap in the flowery curtains and the moon was beaming down brightly into the room. Her bedside lamp was still on and she listened to see if she could hear her granny downstairs. The house was silent.

She closed her eyes and then a sound reached her ears. She sat up and listened. It was the faint sound of birds twittering and water splashing.

She climbed out of her warm bed and tip-toed across the room. When she opened the bedroom door, she gasped in amazement. Instead of the upstairs corridor in her granny's old house, an enchanted forest spread out in front of her.

Without thinking, she stepped from the bedroom and walked onto the warm, narrow pathway. The sun shone through the trees that towered high overhead.

There were flowers of every colour growing here and there. Lucy had never seen flowers like them. For one thing, some weren't just one colour. She had seen red roses, yellow daisies and purple lavender, but she had never seen a flower that changed its colour. One moment they were orange, the next they became bright green. It was as if the flower couldn't make up its mind.

She had decided it would be best not to leave the path, but then off to one side, she saw a creature that made her heart do loop-the-loops. Standing, with its head down, munching on the long grass was a beautiful white unicorn.

Lucy stood like a statue and stared. The horn on the unicorn's head was a spiral and glittered in the sunlight. Suddenly, the creature raised its head and stared straight into the little girl's face.

"Hi!"

Lucy expected the unicorn to dash off, but it didn't. It stood rigid and moved its head as if trying to figure out what sort of animal this little girl was.

Lucy left the path and stepped onto the grass. It felt cool and warm all at once and when she reached the unicorn, she stared up into its big dark eyes.

For a moment nothing happened, then quite unexpectedly, the unicorn lay on the ground next to her.

"Oh, I don't know if I should!" she said, "I've never ridden on a horse before!"

The unicorn made a funny little snort, that almost sounded like laughter and so Lucy reached forward and climbed onto its back. It stood up and Lucy felt as if she was standing on the shoulders of a giant. But she didn't feel scared. The animal seemed so caring and she knew she would be safe.

Off they trotted through the woods and soon that sound of water splashing that had woken her up returned again. It grew louder and louder and as they turned a corner, they reached the edge of a beautiful pale blue lake.

143

In the water, someone was jumping about, having a whale of a time. The unicorn gave a sound and the someone in the lake turned and stared at Lucy.

"Hello!" called Lucy and the little head of the swimmer dropped under the surface of the water.

Lucy climbed down off the back of the unicorn and by the time she had done so, she turned and there on a rock nearby, sat a very wet, tiny little boy. At least, at first Lucy thought it was a boy.

"Are you a fairy?" she asked, amazed at seeing his delicate silvery wings.

"What are you?" the fairy asked.

"What do you mean? I'm a little girl!" replied Lucy.

The fairy stood up and with a flutter of his wings, he flew across toward her.

"Little girls don't exist!" he replied, suspiciously. "Are you a weird sort of goblin?"

"No!" Lucy was so offended and turned back toward the unicorn.

"Sorry!" called the fairy. "It's just . . . well, we've been told that little children, boys and girls, stopped existing long ago!"

"Who told you that?" Lucy asked, very curious.

"Jadel. The witch! She told everyone that the last child grew up and there aren't any more. And so . . . well, we stopped going to see them. We used to go into gardens and hide in sunflowers, or buttercups or fly on the backs of bees and just watch the children play. It was such a nice thing to do. But Jadel told us that if we tried doing that now, the grown-ups would catch us!"

"Well, it's not true. I am a child and I have lots of friends, just like me!"

"Oh, this is so skidoodly. I want to snip-snabble like a wackadoodle!" replied the fairy, flying around Lucy in a circle.

"What are you talking about?" she replied.

"I am so happy, little girl!"

"Where are all the others? Bring me to them. I'll tell them too!"

At hearing this, the little fairy became sad and landed on a lowering tree branch near to Lucy's face.

"They're mostly all gone!"

"Who are?"

"Us!" explained the fairy. "All the fairies, the pixies, the goblins and elves. Very few left. We have to keep hidden."

"Why?" asked Lucy.

"Jadel. She takes us."

"Where?" Lucy had a feeling this Jadel was a big bully and needed her bottom smacked!

"She takes us to her castle. Them that go, never come back!"

The plan was simple. The fairy – whose name was Bibble – would take Lucy to the witch's castle and she would rescue the other creatures. Bibble didn't know how a little girl could do such a daring thing, but Lucy was determined.

The unicorn galloped through the fields and over hedges and dashed through rivers and jumped down rocky hills. Lucy felt as if a pair of arms were holding her safely on the back of the animal and not once did she wobble and feel as if she were about to topple off.

Finally, the castle of the witch came into sight. It was tall and dark and had spikey towers rising high above. The sky over it was filled with smoke and dragons flew around it, as if on guard.

However, when Lucy clip-clopped

up toward the castle gate, the dragons didn't seem to notice. Bibble was very nervous and stood on Lucy's shoulder, hiding himself under her flowing hair.

"Stop!" Lucy whispered and the unicorn immediately did as he was told.

Lucy climbed down and stroked the mane on the animal.

"Wait here and get ready to run!"

The unicorn seemed to understand and stood still. Seeing a light coming from one of the windows, Lucy crossed the courtyard and found a stone. She took aim and threw it. The window smashed, noisily.

Inside the room, a voice screamed and almost immediately a face appeared at the broken glass.

"That's her!" gasped Bibble.

As the witch rushed into the courtyard, Lucy nodded to the unicorn, who took his cue and bolted away from the castle.

"Get him!" screamed the witch and out of nowhere, a broomstick zipped toward her.

She plopped her bottom onto the handle and she flew off after the unicorn.

"Let's go!" whispered Lucy and she ran across the courtyard and entered the first door she came to.

The castle corridors were lit by candles dotted along on the walls. It seemed such a big castle and she now began to feel that perhaps she had not thought the plan through.

"I hear them!" called Bibble, who held onto her hair and flew next to her ear. "This way!"

Lucy ran along corridor after corridor. Then, down a flight of windy stairs and finally came to a huge wooden door.

"In there!" Bibble was so excited.

Lucy reached out and heaved her shoulder against the doors. They creaked open and she slipped into the room.

It was a vast room, with many shelves on all the walls. On each shelf was a cage and in each cage was someone Bibble knew.

"Bibble!" they all called.

Lucy could hardly believe she was in a room filled with fairies, elves and creatures she had only ever heard about in books. It made her sad and a little angry to see them all caged up like that.

"The key!" several of the voices called and she looked to where they were pointing. A key hung from a hook on the wall and so, she ran from cage to cage with it, unlocking them all.

As they were being released, Bibble told them that Lucy was a child and there were many more like her.

Soon, the room was filled with tiny creatures, flitting back and forth, bursting with joy.

"They're so happy, they're snip-snabbling!" explained Bibble.

"Like a wackadoodle?" asked Lucy, to which Bibble nodded and laughed.

"Let's go!" called a goblin and the creatures ran and flew out of the room.

Soon they tumbled out into the light and were crossing the courtyard, heading for the castle gates. But, just as they were about to go through, a gust of wind pushed them back.

Lucy looked up and above in the sky, the dragons flapped hard, stopping them from leaving.

Through the clouds of dust being whipped up, the figure of the witch emerged. She held up her hands and the dragons stopped flapping.

"What is the meaning of this?" she called. Her voice was like ice. "Who is responsible for this outrage?"

"I am!"

Lucy stepped forward and the witch realised straight away that she had been caught out on her lie about there being no more children in the world.

"Why have you caged these creatures? It isn't nice!" called Lucy.

Suddenly, something appeared in the witch's face. It was a look of deep sadness.

"I only wanted a friend!" she said quietly.

"A funny way of showing it!" replied Lucy, sternly.

"It's always the same!" explained Jadel. "Every time I make a friend, they go off and find another friend and leave me!"

"You just wanted us to have one friend!" called a very cross Pixie.

"Yes!" agreed an old Elf, "You didn't want us having another friend, apart from you!"

"You always liked them more than me!" cried the witch.

"No!" replied a very beautiful fairy. "That's what you thought. You were wrong!"

Lucy stepped forward and took the witch's hand. She looked up into the old woman's, sad crumpled face.

"You have to learn to share friends!" she told the witch. "I have friends. Sometimes, I play with one and not the other, but that doesn't mean I don't like them all."

"Do you like carrots?" asked a goblin, stepping up to the witch.

"Yes!" she replied.

"Okay!" continued the goblin. "Do you like cabbage?"

"Yes!" replied Jadel, getting more and more confused.

"Well, if you eat cabbage one day and not have carrots, does that mean you don't like carrots?"

The witch thought for a moment and understood what the strange little goblin was saying.

"No, it's just that I like to have a change now and then!"

"You don't put friends in cages!" replied Lucy, tenderly.

The witch smiled down at the little girl.

"I won't!" Jadel answered and immediately was surrounded by the cheering creatures. Everyone was as happy as the happiest wackadoodle.

Lucy was led back through the forest and the fairies sang songs in celebration. Finally, up ahead on the path, a door appeared. It seemed strangely familiar to Lucy. Then she realised it was the door to her bedroom.

"We've made you a gift!" called Bibble.

From above, four fairies fluttered down, carrying a crown made from flowers and placed it gently on her head.

"You're our Queen!" they called and everyone cheered.

Several of the fairies flew in circles around Lucy. They flew quite close to her face and went so fast, that Lucy closed her eyes.

When she opened her eyes again, the fairies were gone. The forest was gone. Lucy looked around and realised she was in her bed. The bedroom door opened and her grandmother stepped into the room.

"You're awake!" she said surprised, sitting on the bed next to Lucy. "Sleep well?"

Lucy nodded her head, a little sad that it had all been a dream.

"Breakfast's on the table!"

Her grandmother tickled under her chin and was about to stand up, when she stopped and gave Lucy an odd look.

"How did you sleep wearing that?"

Lucy reached up and felt something on her head. She took hold of it and held it in front of her face. It was a crown made from flowers. She smiled like the happiest wackadoodle. Perhaps it hadn't been a dream after all.

Good night
Sleep tight
And no farting!

Printed in Great Britain
by Amazon

55382810R00102